The Fox and the Hen

Eric Battut

Boxer Books

One morning Henrietta Hen laid her very first egg.

"I wonder what this is," she said to herself.

Then along came Red Fox.

"What a nice egg!" he said.
"Would you like to trade it for this tasty, juicy worm?"

"Oh, yes please," said Henrietta Hen,
and she gave her egg to Red Fox.

When the other animals on the farm heard what Henrietta had done, they couldn't believe their ears!

"Oh, Henrietta," said Goose. "Your egg is precious.
You need to look after it and keep it warm.
Red Fox will eat it!"

Henrietta Hen felt very sad. She should never have given away her beautiful egg.

"Don't worry," said Cow. "We'll find a way to get it back."

So Henrietta Hen and Rabbit went to see Red Fox.

"Red Fox," said Henrietta Hen, "would you like to trade that egg for these seeds from Rabbit's garden? They will grow into beautiful, colorful vegetables."

"No, thank you," said Red Fox. "I don't have a garden. And anyway, I'd much rather have a hard-boiled egg for my breakfast."

So Henrietta Hen tried again. This time, Goose came along.

"Red Fox," she said, "would you like to trade that egg
for some beautiful white feathers from Goose?
They will make a soft and fluffy pillow for your bed.
What do you say?"

"No need," said Red Fox. "My bed is already nice and soft.
Besides, I'd rather have a soft poached egg."

Henrietta Hen went away and thought hard.
Then she went back to Red Fox with Goat.

"Red Fox," she said, "would you like to exchange that egg for this delicious cheese from Goat? It's soft and creamy and oh, so yummy!"

"Absolutely not," said Red Fox. "I already have plenty of cheese. And anyway, I'm in the mood for an omelet."

But Henrietta didn't give up. Back she went with Sheep.

"Red Fox," she said, "would you like to trade that egg for this beautiful wool from Sheep? It will make a cozy sweater to keep you warm in winter."

"Out of the question," said Red Fox. "I already have a furry red coat to keep me warm. Besides, I'd prefer a scrambled egg."

So Henrietta tried again. Pig came with her.

"Red Fox," she said, "would you like to trade that egg for this nice jar of marmalade that Pig has made?"

"Oh, no," said Red Fox. "I can't stand marmalade. I'd much rather have a delicious fried egg for breakfast."

But still Henrietta Hen did not give up. She and Cow went back to see Red Fox one more time.

"Red Fox," she said, "would you like to trade that egg for some delicious, creamy milk from Cow?"

"No way," said Red Fox. "I don't want any milk. I'm going to have a yummy soft-boiled egg instead."

Henrietta Hen didn't know what to do! How would she get her beautiful egg back? All the animals thought very, very hard.

Suddenly Henrietta Hen had an idea.
"We need to find an egg even bigger and more beautiful than mine!" she said. "Red Fox will never be able to refuse that."

The animals looked all over the farm until they found an enormous stone. Then they painted it carefully with some white paint. It really did look like a gigantic egg!

Then Henrietta Hen ran straight back to Red Fox.

"Look what I found!" she said, showing Red Fox the giant egg. "Would you like to trade that teeny tiny egg for this great big one?"

"Oh, yes!" said Red Fox, licking his chops.

So Henrietta picked up her very small, very precious egg and carried it carefully home.

When Henrietta got back to the farm, her egg began to wobble and wiggle and shake, and a little yellow chick stuck its head out of the top.

Henrietta was the happiest hen in the world.

And what about Red Fox?

Well, he quickly built a fire, put the giant egg
in a giant pot, and waited impatiently to enjoy
his giant hard-boiled egg.

But that giant egg turned out to be a whole
lot harder than Red Fox expected.

THE END

First American edition published in 2010 by Boxer Books Limited.

Distributed in the United States and Canada by
Sterling Publishing Co., Inc. 387 Park Avenue South, New York, NY 10016-8810

First published in Great Britain in 2010 by Boxer Books Limited.
www.boxerbooks.com

The illustrations were prepared using acrylic paints. The text is set in Adobe Garamond Pro.

ISBN 978-1-907152-02-3

1 3 5 7 9 10 8 6 4 2

Printed in China

All of our papers are sourced from managed forests and renewable resources.